ou

ould eat if you went

or tea with a mermaid?

Sea cucumbers and
sea tomatoes.
– Frankie

Soggy sandwiches.
Yum yum!
– Ruby

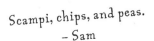

Scampi, chips, and peas.
– Sam

Mercakes and merbiscuits!
– Harriet

Waterproof crisps.
– Oliver

Fish food?
– Antonia

Family Tree

My Mum
Countess Cordelia
Moon

Baby Honeyblossom

My Dad
Count Bartholomew
Moon

Me!
Isadora Moon

Pink Rabbit

For vampires, fairies and humans everywhere!

And for Erin Green, dolphin queen.

OXFORD

UNIVERSITY PRESS

Great Clarendon Street, Oxford OX2 6DP

Oxford University Press is a department of the University of Oxford.
It furthers the University's objective of excellence in research, scholarship, and
education by publishing worldwide. Oxford is a registered trade mark of Oxford
University Press in the UK and in certain other countries

First published 2016

British Library Cataloguing in Publication Data

Data available

ISBN: 978-0-19-274433-3

1 3 5 7 9 10 8 6 4 2

Printed in Great Britain by Bell and Bain Ltd, Glasgow

Paper used in the production of this book is a natural,
recyclable product made from wood grown in sustainable forests.
The manufacturing process conforms to the environmental
regulations of the country of origin.

MIX
Paper from
responsible sources
FSC
www.fsc.org
FSC® C007785

ISADORA · MOON

Goes Camping

Harriet Muncaster

OXFORD
UNIVERSITY PRESS

Chapter ONE

Isadora Moon, that's me! And my best friend is Pink Rabbit. He was my favourite toy so Mum magicked him alive with her magic wand. Mum can do things like that because she is a fairy. Oh, and did I also mention that my dad is a vampire? That makes me half fairy, half vampire!

My second best friends are Zoe and Oliver. We all go to the same school together. It's a regular school for human children. I love it!

Every morning Zoe and Oliver knock for me and we walk to school together. Mum and Dad always try and avoid opening the door. They are still a bit funny about talking to humans.

It was the first day back at school after the summer holidays and I was really looking forward to seeing my friends. As soon as I heard a 'Bang bang bang' on the door, I flew to open it.

'Zoe!' I said leaping on top of her and giving her a big hug. I didn't leap on top of Oliver because he doesn't like hugs.

We started to walk down the garden
path together and Pink Rabbit bounced
along beside us. Zoe made a tinkling
sound as she walked because she was

wearing a lot of jewellery. She wants to be an actress when she grows up and is always dressing up as different people.

'Today I am the Queen!' she told me, twizzling one of her necklaces round her finger and patting the paper crown on her head. 'Queen Zoe!'

'I like your bracelets,' I said. 'Where did you get them?'

'In France!' said Zoe. 'That's where we went on holiday. It was *très* fantastic. We went there on a ferry boat.'

'Ooh that sounds great,' said Oliver. He loves boats.

Then she fished in her bag and pulled out another bracelet.

'This one's for you Isadora,' she said. 'From France.'

'Wow!' I said, taking the bracelet. 'Thanks Zoe!' I felt all glowy inside as I put it on.

'And this is for you Oliver,' said Zoe holding out a magnet in the shape of the French flag.

'Cool!' said Oliver. 'Thanks Zoe.'

It was very kind of Zoe to bring me something from her holiday but I felt a tiny bit embarrassed that I hadn't got anything for her.

'I can't wait for show and tell today,' said Oliver. 'I've brought photos of my holiday. We stayed in a hotel by the seaside!'

'That sounds nice,' I said and then I tried to change the subject. I suddenly didn't want to talk about holidays anymore. Especially my holiday. I had been to the seaside like Zoe and Oliver but strange things had happened there . . . the sort of things that probably didn't happen on human holidays.

When we got to school our teacher, Miss Cherry, was already arranging the classroom for show and tell.

'Good morning everyone!' she said, beaming round the classroom. 'I hope you all had a wonderful summer. Who wants to come up and talk about their holiday first?'

A forest of hands shot up into the air and I tried to slink down behind my desk. I really didn't want to stand up and tell everyone about my holiday. I was sure they would all think my holiday was not normal. I felt embarrassed.

'Isadora Moon!' said Miss Cherry. 'How about you?'

I stared at her in panic.

'Come on,' she said. 'I'm sure you had a lovely summer.'

Slowly I stood up and walked to the front of the class. A sea of expectant faces stared back at me. I took a deep breath and felt my voice wobble.

'Well…' I began.

It all started one sunny morning. I came downstairs to find Mum waving her wand about in the kitchen. She had magicked up a flowery-patterned tent and it was sitting in the middle of the floor. My baby sister, Honeyblossom, was in her high-chair mashing toast into her face, and Dad

17

was sitting at the table with her, yawning (he had just come back from his nightly fly), and drinking his red juice. Dad only ever drinks red juice. It's a vampire thing.

Mum smiled at me as I came into the room. 'There you are!' she said. 'What do you think of this?' She pointed at the tent. 'Do you like the pattern? It's for you. We're going camping!'

'WHAT!?' said Dad.

'Camping!' Mum repeated. 'We're going camping by the sea. I booked it this morning.'

'I,' said Dad primly, 'do not *do* camping.'

'Oh don't be silly!' said Mum. 'You'll

love it! There's nothing better than waking up outdoors with the morning sunshine blasting into your tent, cooking on a campfire, playing on the beach. It's wonderful to be so close to nature!'

Dad did not look convinced.

I walked round the tent in the middle of the floor inspecting it and lifting the flap to peer inside.

'So what do you think?' asked Mum again.

'I'm not sure about the colour,' I admitted. 'It's a bit *too* pink and flowery…'

'OK,' said Mum. 'How about this.' She waved her wand again and the tent

changed to a black and white stripy pattern.

'Ooh yes, that's more like it.' I said, crawling inside. Pink Rabbit followed me and we sat crouched under the canvas walls listening to Mum and Dad.

'We'll be right next to the beach so we can go swimming in the sea every day,' Mum was saying. Pink Rabbit put his paws over his ears. He hates getting wet because it takes him ages to get dry. We have to peg him up outside on the washing line.

'And anyway,' Mum said. 'It's booked. It's final. We're going camping. We leave this afternoon. So you'd better get packing!'

'Well then,' said Dad. 'I'm going up for a bath. To enjoy my home comforts while I still can.'

I did wonder how Dad was going to cope without his bathroom on our camping trip. He does like to spend a lot of time in there. He has baths that last for hours where he plays classical music and lights hundreds of flickering candles. Then he spends at least an hour with his special comb, smoothing down his shiny black hair with gel.

'A vampire's hair is their pride and joy,' he always says. 'You ought to brush yours more often.'

After breakfast we all went to pack our things and then stood by the front door waiting for Dad. Eventually he appeared at the top of the stairs with five giant suitcases.

'You can't bring all that!' Mum gasped. 'It won't fit in the car!'

'We'll strap it onto the roof then,' said Dad cheerfully.

Mum sighed. She tried to pick up one of the suitcases but it was so heavy she couldn't even get it off the ground.

'What *have* you got in there?' she said, waving her wand at it. The suitcase sprang open and hundreds of Dad's grooming products burst out onto the floor.

Mum rolled her eyes. She pointed at a twirly black comb. 'Surely you're not bringing that,' she said. 'That's your great-great-great-grandfather's antique jewelled vampire comb.'

'Yes, and it's my favourite thing!' Dad said.

'But that comb is very precious,' said Mum, helping Dad to put everything back into the suitcase. 'You don't want to lose it.'

'I won't lose it,' said Dad picking it up and admiring the red rubies which sparkled in the handle. 'Look how it shines.'

Dad's suitcases took up so much space that there was barely room for Pink Rabbit, Honeyblossom, and me to sit in the back. It wasn't very comfortable.

It was a very long drive. Pink Rabbit kept bouncing up and down on my lap trying to spot the sea out of the window. Bounce, bounce, bounce. And then at last, BOUNCE!

Because finally there it was. The blue sparkling sea, like a glittering ribbon across the horizon.

'THE SEA!' I shouted. 'There's the sea! We're here!'

Honeyblossom waved her little chubby arms in approval.

Mum started humming as she

drove the car down a bumpy countryside lane. Pink Rabbit and I stared out of the window. At the end of the lane there was a sign. It read:

Welcome to Mermaid Bay campsite

'That's us!' said Mum cheerfully, driving past the sign and into a small field with lots of tents in it.

'Isn't it just lovely!' said Mum as we parked up and got out of the car. 'Breathe in that lovely sea air Isadora!'

I took a long sniff. So did Pink Rabbit.

It smelt salty and fresh.

    Mum magicked the tents up. The one
Mum, Dad, and Honeyblossom were sharing
was really huge. And not *usual* looking.

'You can always come into our tent if you get scared in the night,' said Mum.

'I won't be scared!' I laughed. 'I am half vampire. I love the night!'

Dad was busy rootling through his suitcases. 'I know I put that bat-patterned wallpaper somewhere,' he muttered. 'And in which suitcase did I put my pop-up four-poster bed? And where on earth am I supposed to plug in my portable fridge?'

By the time we were all unpacked it was dark. Mum and I made a campfire and we all sat round it toasting marshmallows on long sticks.

'Isn't this wonderful?' said Mum. 'This is what camping is all about!'

I nodded. My
mouth was full of
gooey marshmallow.
Even Dad seemed to have
perked up a bit since the sun had
gone down. He sucked on the straw
of his carton of red juice and stared
up at the sky.

'You can see more stars now that
we're in the countryside,' said Dad.
He leapt up to go and fetch his special
astronomer's telescope from
their tent.

'I'm going to
stargaze all night!'
he said happily.

'Not all night,' said Mum. 'You need to get some sleep so we can have a day at the beach tomorrow.'

'But vampires are awake at night and sleep in the day! It's what we do,' he gasped.

'Just try it,' said Mum.

Dad sighed.

'I'll try,' he promised.

Chapter TWO

When you are camping you have to walk to a place called 'The Toilet Block' in your pyjamas, to brush your teeth and have a shower. I had to brush my teeth at a basin next to other people staying on the campsite. It felt a bit funny wearing my pyjamas in public but it didn't matter because everyone else was wearing them too!

We had to use Mum's wand as a torch to walk back across the field after brushing our teeth. Then Pink Rabbit

and I crawled into our
stripy tent and snuggled
up in the sleeping bag
together. It was very cosy.
Dad zipped the door up tight
for us.

'Goodnight Isadora,' he
said. 'Goodnight Pink Rabbit.'

'Goodnight,' I yawned.

Then I lay there in the dark for a bit.
There were strange noises all around.
Things rustling, owls hooting, people
talking. But I wasn't scared.
I love the
dark!

I woke up early the next morning because the sun was shining brightly on the roof of my tent. It was very hot.

'Good morning,' chirped Mum when I poked my head outside. 'We're going to the beach as soon as you're ready. We just need to find Dad first. He's disappeared off somewhere . . .'

I had an idea of where Dad might be.

Outside the one shower cubicle in The Toilet Block there was a long queue of grumbling people. I skipped past all of them and knocked on the door.

'Dad?' I said.

'Yes.'

'How long have you been in there?'

'Only a couple of hours.'

A cloud of warm steam rose up from under the door and Dad started humming contentedly.

'Dad,' I said again. 'There's a big queue of people waiting you know.'

'Is there?' said Dad, sounding surprised.

'*Yes*,' I said. 'You need to hurry up. We're going to the beach.'

I heard the shower turn off.

'Alright,' he said. 'I'm coming.'

Dad appeared in his towel and turban. He looked very refreshed.

We walked back along the queue of people and I felt my cheeks turn pink with embarrassment. They were all staring at Dad and they didn't look very happy.

'There you are!' said Mum when we got back to the tent. 'Now we can go to the beach!'

'I'm not ready *yet*,' said Dad. 'Just give me five minutes.'

Half an hour later Dad emerged from the tent, wearing his black cape and sunglasses with a black parasol tucked under his arm. He was also holding a pot of hair gel and his great-great-great-grandfather's precious antique vampire comb.

'I'm ready!' Dad grinned.

We went through a little gate in the side of the camping field and walked down a sandy path to the beach. Mum spread out a picnic blanket and sat down.

'Isn't it wonderful!' she said.

It was pretty wonderful. The sea was blue and sparkly and the sand was warm and tickly between my toes.

'Come and build a sandcastle with me Dad!' I said.

'OK! Just give me five minutes,' Dad said. He put up his big black umbrella and slathered himself with factor sixty sun cream. Then he wrapped himself in his black cape and got out his comb.

'You must be hot Dad,' I said to him, as I started building a sandcastle nearby.

Dad shook his head.

'I am not hot,' he insisted as sweat began to drip down his face. He started to do his hair, smoothing big gloops of gel into it.

By the time Dad was done combing and smoothing his hair, I had finished building my sandcastle. It was a very big one with lots of turrets. Pink Rabbit and I walked along the beach collecting shells. We poked them into the castle walls for decoration.

'It needs something else,' I said to him when we had placed them all.

'It needs something on the top to just finish it off.'

I glanced over to where Dad was now snoozing under the parasol and an idea crept into my head.

'Dad won't notice if we borrow the jewelled comb for just ten minutes,' I whispered to Pink Rabbit. We tiptoed over and I picked up the comb. It really was very beautiful. The rubies in the handle flashed in the sunlight. I pressed it down into the very top of the highest castle turret and stood back to admire my handiwork.

I glanced back at Dad but he was still asleep.

'Isadora,' Mum called over.

'Do you want to go in the sea with me and Honeyblossom?'

'Yes, please!' I shouted excitedly.

So we put Honeyblossom in her rubber ring, and went down to the shore.

'Come on Dad!' I called. 'It's nice and cool in the water!'

But Dad was still asleep under the umbrella and didn't hear me. I thought it was a shame. I know Dad quite enjoys swimming. He is the one who takes me to my Little Vampires swimming lessons every week. We always have lots of fun in the pool together. He has been trying to teach me to swim underwater though I haven't quite managed it yet.

'This is lovely!' said Mum splashing about in the waves with Honeyblossom.

Honeyblossom waved her little arms and kicked her little feet. She opened her mouth and squealed with happiness…

…and her dummy dropped into the water.

'Oh no!' said Mum, trying to catch it.

I watched as the dummy began to sink slowly down to the bottom of the sea. Honeyblossom started to wail.

'Oh no!' said Mum again.

'WAAAAAAHH!' screamed Honeyblossom.

I decided I would be brave. I held my breath, scrunched up my eyes, and then I put my head *under the water!*

All I could hear was the roar of the

sea, and when I peeped my eyes open everything was hazy and green. I pushed my arms out in front of me and reached for the dummy.

'Isadora!' shouted Mum in an excited voice when I popped my head back up a few seconds later. 'You just swam underwater!'

I held the dummy up in the air like a trophy.

'I did it!' I yelled.

'Well done,' said Mum, smiling proudly. 'That's a real achievement!'

'I wish Dad had seen it,' I said.

By the time we got out of the sea the
tide had come in and my sandcastle had
disappeared under the water and Dad was
busy packing away all our things.

'I'm sure I brought it,' he muttered.

'What have you lost?' Mum asked.

'My comb!' replied Dad. 'My great-
great-great-grandfather's precious antique
vampire comb!'

I froze. Suddenly my whole body felt cold even though it was a warm day. I stared out to the spot where my sandcastle had been. I had forgotten to take Dad's comb off the top of my castle and now it had been washed away!

'Dad…' I began. But the words wouldn't come out of my mouth.

'I'm sure I had it,' Dad was saying, scratching his head in confusion. 'It was right HERE.'

'It can't have gone far,' Mum said, as she started to poke around in the sand where Dad had been sitting.

'It's been stolen!' Dad howled.

'Nonsense,' said Mum. 'Who on earth

could have
stolen it?'

'A crab?'
Dad sniffed.
'A sneaky little crab!'

'That's not *very* likely,' said Mum.
'It must be somewhere around here. Let
me try a spell.'

She waved her wand but the comb
did not appear.

'That's funny,' Mum frowned. 'My
magic usually works.'

I felt so guilty that my stomach hurt
but I couldn't seem to get the words out
of my mouth to tell Dad that his comb
was lost...

We all walked back up the beach towards the campsite. Dad's mouth was turned down at the edges. He did not look happy.

'We will have to tell him soon,' I whispered to Pink Rabbit. 'Maybe after dinner, at bedtime. He might be more cheerful when he's had his red juice.'

Pink Rabbit nodded. He knows it is best to always be honest.

'I'm really sorry about your comb Dad,' I blurted out when he came to tuck us in at bedtime.

'It's not your fault Isadora,' Dad smiled sadly. 'I'm sure it will turn up.'

I took a deep breath.

'Actually…' I began. But Dad had turned his head because Mum was calling him.

'I'd better go,' he said. 'Goodnight Isadora.'

'Goodnight,' I whispered.

Chapter THREE

Pink Rabbit and I lay in the dark. I felt so bad about the comb that I couldn't sleep.

It was lost forever at the bottom of the deep blue sea!

Or was it?

I sat up in bed. Was there a chance that the comb could have washed back up on the sand?

I scrambled out of my sleeping bag and crawled towards the opening of our tent.

'Pink Rabbit!' I whispered. 'Wake up! We're going to the beach.'

Pink Rabbit bounced out of bed. I don't think he had been able to sleep either. Together we crept out of the tent and stood in the dark field. The sky was full of stars and all we could hear were the faint sounds of people snoring.

I tiptoed over to Mum and Dad's tent.

'We'll need Mum's wand for a torch,' I whispered to Pink Rabbit as I silently slid it out of her bag. I waved it in the air and the star immediately glowed pink. I reached down for Pink Rabbit's paw and together we flapped up into the air.

I love to fly, especially at night. We soared up high over the field until all the tents were just black little specks. Then we swooped down towards the beach and the sound of the roaring sea.

I pointed Mum's torch down at the sand.

'It might have washed up around here,' I said hopefully.

We walked up and down the shoreline, squinting in the pink wand-light. Little bits of sea glass and pearly shells winked up at us but none of them were Dad's comb. Pink Rabbit held on to my hand tightly. He finds the darkness a bit too mysterious sometimes.

Suddenly there came a small splashing sound from the sea.

I stared at Pink Rabbit.

'What was that?' I whispered.

Pink Rabbit didn't know because he had his paws over his eyes.

I peered out to sea. There was something shining and sparkling in the water. Maybe it was Dad's comb! I rose up into the air, pulling Pink Rabbit behind me.

'Come on!' I said to him. 'Let's look!'

We fluttered towards the shining thing in the sea. As we got closer I could see that it was moving. 'It can't be the comb,' I said to Pink Rabbit. We flew a little closer and heard a soft tinkly voice calling out.

'Hello?'

I could see that there was a girl about my age in the sea. She had long, long hair and a gleaming fish tail that kept flicking in and out of the water. I hovered above her, holding Pink Rabbit clear of the waves.

'Are you a mermaid?' I asked.

'Yes,' she said in a song-like voice. 'How are you floating up there?'

'I'm flying, not floating! I am half vampire, half fairy.' I turned in the air to show her my wings.

'I've never met a half vampire, half fairy before!' she said.

'I've never met a mermaid before!' I replied.

We both laughed. She had a laugh
that sounded like strings of shells tinkling
in the breeze.

'My name's Marina. What's yours?'

'Isadora.' I said. Then I pointed at
Pink Rabbit. 'This is Pink Rabbit.'

'He's funny,' she giggled, reaching out
and poking his stomach.

Pink Rabbit stiffened. He doesn't like
to be called funny.

'What are you doing out here so late
at night?' Marina asked.

'I was looking for something really
precious. It got lost here today while we
were at the beach.'

'Oh?' Marina said. 'What is it?'

'A comb.' I said. 'A really special comb. It's my Dad's.'

'Was it black?' Marina asked. 'With twirly designs on it? And rubies?'

'Yes!' I said hopefully. 'Have you seen it?!'

'I have…' said Marina, 'but…'

'Where is it?' I asked excitedly. 'I need it back!'

Marina looked a bit worried.

'The Mermaid Princess has it,' she said. 'All the nicest jewels found on the beach always go to the Mermaid Princess. She doesn't like to share.'

'But it's my Dad's comb,' I said in a panicky voice. 'I need it back.' I felt my eyes fill with tears.

Marina bit her lip. 'It's a bit tricky,' she said. 'There are different rules for under the sea you know. It's finders keepers here.'

I wiped my eyes and sniffed.

'I'll tell you what,' said Marina. 'Why don't I take you to the Mermaid Princess? You can ask her yourself! Maybe she'll let you have it back if you explain.'

I felt Pink Rabbit tug at my hand in fright. He hates the water.

'It's not far to the palace,' said Marina. 'Just follow me. Come on!'

I stared at the water, now black under the night sky.

'I *can* swim underwater now,'
I told Marina proudly. 'But I can't hold
my breath for very long. How can we
follow you?'

Marina laughed her tinkly laugh
again.

'Silly me!' she
said. 'I forgot!
Just wear this so
you can breathe
underwater. It's
magical.' She handed
me a necklace made of shells and
I put it on.

'What about Pink Rabbit? He hates
getting wet.'

70

'Hmm,' Marina said thinking hard. 'I know!' She splashed her tail in the water to make some bubbles on the surface and then she lifted one of the bubbles out of the water on the tip of her finger and blew on it. It got bigger and bigger until it was big enough for Pink Rabbit to pop inside. Then she held out her hand to me.

'Come on,' she said. 'Let's go.'

I smiled, trying to show I was
not afraid and let her pull me down
towards the water. It was cold at first
and I gasped.

'You'll get used to it,' Marina said.

Everything under the water gleamed
in the moonlight. The seaweed swayed
gently below us and little silver fishes

darted in and out. I was surprised to find
that I could breathe as easily as if
I had been on land. I glanced back over
my shoulder to check that Pink Rabbit
was alright in his bubble.

Marina pointed to a silhouette in
the distance.

'There's the palace,' she said. 'It's not
far at all!'

'You can speak underwater!' I said in surprise. And then I put my hand to my mouth. 'So can I!' I said in wonder.

Marina laughed again.

'That's because you're wearing the magic necklace,' she explained. 'And of course I can speak underwater, I'm a mermaid!'

We swam further on towards the silhouette. Now it was getting closer, and I could make out spires and turrets looming up towards the surface of the water. It was very pretty, with shells stuck all round the walls just like my sandcastle!

'Here we are,' said Marina. She heaved open the gigantic front door and invited me

into a cavernous entrance hall lit by twinkly lights. Even the walls were studded with shiny jewels and pearls.

'Wow!' I said, gazing round. 'It's so beautiful!'

Marina led us through to another huge room, with a silver throne in the middle. And on the throne sat the Mermaid Princess. I could tell she was the princess because she was wearing a crown. On her lap there was a teddy bear, but instead of legs it had a fish tail like a mermaid. The Princess was busy combing its fur… with Dad's great-great-great-grandfather's special comb!

The Princess looked up when we

swam into the room. Everything about her sparkled. She had pearls and starfish in her hair and rows of jewelled bracelets on her arms. Round her neck were about ten pearl necklaces which all shimmered and glimmered in the undersea light.

Marina gave a small cough. 'Your Highness,' she said. 'I have brought someone to see you.'

'What is this?' The princess said, sounding puzzled. 'You don't have a tail!'

'No,' I said. 'But I do have wings! I am a vampire fairy. I'm Isadora Moon and this is Pink Rabbit.'

'I see,' said the Princess, glancing interestedly at Pink Rabbit. 'My name

is Delphina. *Princess* Delphina. One day
I shall be Queen of the Sea!' I smiled
nervously.

'There was actually something
I wanted to talk to you about,' I said.

'That comb you're holding, I was wondering if I could please have it back? I lost it today on the beach. It's my Dad's and it's his very special favourite thing. He's very upset about losing it.'

Princess Delphina's eyes glittered.

'But I like it. It's so sparkly.' She held it up in the water so that the rubies flashed in the glowing lights.

'Yes, but it's not really yours to keep,' I said.

'Well, I suppose you could have the comb back…if you stay for tea.'

'Oh,' I said, surprised. 'OK. Of course we will stay for tea!'

Chapter
FOUR

So Pink Rabbit and Marina and I had tea
together with Princess Delphina and her
mer-bear. We had cupcakes and sea berries
and little shrimp sandwiches with the crusts
cut off. It was all very nice, but everything
tasted a bit soggy.

'That was lovely,' I said politely. 'Thank
you. Could I please have the comb now?'

Princess Delphina frowned.

'I will give it to you,' she said. 'If you play a game of hide and seek with me.'

'But…' I began.

'I'll count!' said the Princess. 'Go and hide!'

So we all played hide and seek for quite a long time and Marina whispered to me that we must always let the Princess win. So we did.

'That was great fun!' said the Princess. 'Let's play something else now!'

I stared upward towards the surface of the water and felt a bit worried. It was starting to get light.

'Let's play… dress up!' said the

82

Mermaid Princess and she led us over to a big box of jewels by her throne. She began to pick out pearl necklaces and coral bracelets and shiny tiaras made of shells and starfish.

'Put these on!' she ordered, holding the jewels out towards me.

'I…' I started to object.

'Oh go on,' the Princess said. 'No one ever comes to play with me.'

I glanced up at the surface of the water again. It was getting lighter by the second.

'I can't,' I said. 'I'm sorry but I really have to go. Can I have the comb back now, please?'

The Princess looked cross and a little bit sad.

'I'll give it to you . . . if you give me Pink Rabbit,' she said.

'Oh no!' I said, shocked. 'I absolutely cannot give you Pink Rabbit. And he would hate living under the sea.'

The Princess looked disappointed and suddenly I knew what the matter was. She was lonely.

'I have an idea,' I said. 'Why don't I try and magic your mer-bear alive for you in exchange for the comb? I have my mum's wand with me. I think I know how to do it.'

The Princess's eyes lit up. She hugged her mer-bear to her chest and then held it out towards me.

'Yes!' she said. 'Yes! If you can make my bear come alive I promise I will give you the comb.'

I held out Mum's wand and pointed it at the bear. Using a magic wand is not my strongest skill but I had to try. I waved it back and forth in the water and a stream of bubbles shot out of the end.

When they cleared the mer-bear
was twitching his head and moving his
paw about.

But still,
something
wasn't quite
right…

Quickly I
waved the wand
again…

And
again…

Until
finally… I got
it right.

'Phew,'
I whispered to Pink
Rabbit. 'That almost
didn't work.'

The Princess
beamed happily as her
mer-bear swam round
her head in circles.

She held out the comb to me.

'Thank you Isadora!' she said. 'Take the comb. It's yours!'

I tucked the comb safely in my pyjama pocket before the Princess could change her mind and then Marina and I said goodbye and left the palace.

As we swam back up towards the surface of the water I could see it was morning.

We reached the surface and I took a big gulp of air. Pink Rabbit's bubble popped and I caught him just before he fell into the water.

Marina smiled at me and
I smiled back.

'It was nice to meet you,' she said.

'It was nice to meet you too,'
I replied. 'Thank you so much for helping
me find my Dad's comb.'

'It was a pleasure,' said Marina in her
tinkly little voice. 'And you've made the
Mermaid Princess very happy.'

I started to take the magic necklace
off.

'Keep it,' said Marina. 'It won't work
again but it's pretty. You can wear it!'

'Thank you,' I said, feeling happy
inside.

Marina glanced at the rising sun.

'I had better go,' she said. 'I don't want to be spotted by any humans. And you had better get back too.'

I nodded and flapped my wings, sending a flurry of water droplets flying as I rose into the air.

'Goodbye Marina!' I said.

'Goodbye Isadora!' she replied. And then with a splash and a laugh, she was gone.

I held Pink Rabbit in my arms and we flew as fast as we could back to the campsite. It was still very early and all was quiet. I snuck into Mum and Dad's tent and slipped the wand into Mum's bag before heading to my own tent to put on some dry clothes. When I poked my head out of my tent again I got the surprise of my life.

Dad was sitting by the campfire! He was wearing a t-shirt and shorts and he was busy making breakfast for everyone.

'There you are Isadora,' he said. 'You're up bright and early!'

'But… but…what are you doing up so early?' I asked.

'It looks like it's going to be a lovely day,' said Dad. 'We're going to the beach again. Last night Mum told me that you swam underwater yesterday. I'm really sorry I missed it. It made me realize that I don't want to miss out on anything else this holiday. I can't wait for you to show me your underwater swimming later!'

'I can't wait to show you!' I said. 'But what about your comb Dad?'

He looked sad for a minute but then he shook his head and shrugged.

'It was a beautiful comb,' he said. 'And very precious. But it was my own fault for bringing it to the beach. I should have left it in the tent. And you know, I've been thinking: spending time with my family is more important than a silly comb. Besides,' he said, running a hand through his sleek hair. 'I've still got my hair gel.'

I took the comb from behind my back and held it out to Dad. His eyes went big and wide and his mouth made an 'O' shape.

'I'm really sorry,' I said, 'but it was me who lost your comb. I put it on my sandcastle and the sea washed it away. But then I went and searched for it and found it! I'm sorry I didn't tell you sooner.'

Dad took the comb and his face
creased up with delight.

'My comb!' he cried, jumping into the air. 'My beloved comb!' He kissed it and ran away into his tent to lock it safely in his suitcase.

When Dad came back, we sat down together next to the campfire.

'You know Isadora,' Dad said. 'I'm glad you found my comb, but honesty is always the best policy. If you had told me you'd lost it, we could have looked for it together.'

'Sorry, Dad,' I said.

Dad gave me a big hug and we cooked breakfast together.

After that it was time to go to the beach and it was the best day ever.

Dad came in the sea and let me ride on his back and then I showed him my underwater swimming, which was loads better after all the practice I had the night before. Dad was very impressed. We all had a picnic together and then we made the biggest, fanciest sandcastle ever!

'Fit for a vampire-fairy-mermaid princess!' Dad said.

That night I felt so happy as we all sat round the campfire eating our dinner. Dad even tried a roasted marshmallow on a stick! Usually he refuses anything but red juice.

'Isadora's underwater swimming was fantastic!' he said. 'I'm so glad I got to see it today.'

I felt prouder than ever as I licked my marshmallow.

Dad put his arms around me and Mum and Honeyblossom and the firelight flickered on our faces. Suddenly I felt very tired.

'You were just like a mermaid!' said Dad as I snuggled into him.

I laughed sleepily. 'Don't be silly Dad,' I said. 'Everyone knows there's no such thing as mermaids!'

Then I turned my head and winked at Pink Rabbit. Moonlight flashed off his button eyes and I could tell he was winking back.

I finished talking and realized that the whole class was staring at me with their mouths wide open. Even Miss Cherry.

'It sounds like you had an amazing holiday Isadora!' she said.

'I want to see a mermaid!' shouted out Zoe.

'I want to toast marshmallows on a campfire!' said Oliver.

'I want to sleep in a tent!' said someone else.

I pulled the shell necklace out from under my uniform.

'This is the necklace the mermaid gave me,' I told the class. I took it off

and held it up in the air so that the shells
tinkled together. It sounded like Marina's
laugh.

'OOH,' they all whispered, their eyes
big and round like saucers. Zoe's eyes were
the biggest of them all. I walked over to
her desk and held out the necklace.

'It's for you,' I said to her. 'A holiday present!'

Zoe beamed.

'How lovely,' said Miss Cherry. Then she looked at her watch. 'My goodness!' she exclaimed. 'Look at the time! We will have to carry on with this after lunch. Thank you, Isadora, for giving us such an interesting account of your holiday.'

I smiled. Suddenly I didn't mind show and tell so much any more.

'I expect your family will be going camping again next year,' said Miss Cherry. 'As you had such a wonderful time this summer.'

'Oh no!' I said in surprise. 'Dad's choosing the holiday next year. We're going to the Nighttime Vampire Hotel. They've got a spa!'

Harriet Muncaster, that's me! I'm the
author and illustrator of Isadora Moon.
Yes really! I love anything teeny tiny,
anything starry, and everything glittery.

What is Isadora up to next . . . ?

ISADORA MOON

Has a Birthday

Half vampire, half fairy, totally unique!

Harriet Muncaster

It's Isadora's birthday, and what she really wants is to have a human party! But with Mum and Dad doing the organizing, things don't quite turn out as she expects.

In this extract, Dad is in charge of the party games ...

Then he produced a big parcel from
behind his back.

'Everyone in a circle, please!' he said.

My friends and I shuffled ourselves
into a circle on the floor and Dad gave the
parcel to one of the children.

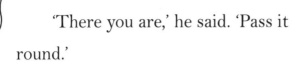

'There you are,' he said. 'Pass it round.'

We all started to pass the parcel round the circle. But something was missing.

'Music!' I whispered to Dad. 'We need music!'

'Music!' shouted Dad to Mum.

Mum opened her mouth and started to sing a tinkly fairy song. I felt my face go red with embarrassment. Some of my friends started to giggle.

'That's right!' called Dad. 'Pass it round. Round and round it goes!'

The parcel went round and round the circle. And round and round again! I started to wonder when Mum was going to stop singing. I was about to whisper to Dad again when suddenly there was an almighty bang.

'SURPRISE!!' shouted Dad as the parcel exploded in Oliver's hands. Fireworks shot out of it and up into the air.

Glittery pink sparks and sparkling fizzing stars swirled and whirled around the room.

'Oh no!' I said to Pink Rabbit.

But my friends didn't seem to mind. In fact, they seemed to like it. They all stood up and started dancing to Mum's song under the falling sparks.

'They're so pretty!' breathed Zoe as she tried to catch a shooting star.

'It's magical!' yelled Sashi.

Everyone danced until the sparks stopped falling and Mum stopped singing.

'Time for the magician,' announced Dad, opening the door for Wilbur. He swept in, swishing his starry robe.

'It's Wilbur the Great, actually,' corrected Wilbur. 'Sit down everyone,' he said bossily. 'Today I am going to show you a wonderful trick. Who wants to be turned into a box of frogs?'

I groaned. A boy from my class called Bruno put his hand in the air and Wilbur gestured for Bruno to come and stand at the front.

Isadora Moon

Isadora Moon
Goes to School

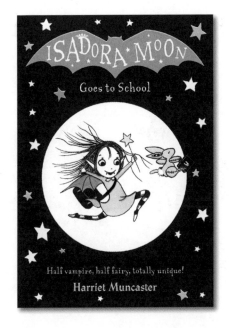

Her mum is a fairy and her dad is a vampire
and she is a bit of both. She loves the night, bats,
and her black tutu, but she also loves the sunshine,
her magic wand, and Pink Rabbit.

When it's time for Isadora to start school
she's not sure where she belongs—fairy school
or vampire school?

Isadora Moon
Has a Birthday

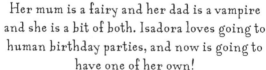

Her mum is a fairy and her dad is a vampire
and she is a bit of both. Isadora loves going to
human birthday parties, and now is going to
have one of her own!

But with her mum and dad organizing things, it's not
going to be like the parties she's been to before. . .

Isadora Moon
Goes to the Ballet

Her mum is a fairy and her dad is a vampire
and she is a bit of both. Isadora loves ballet,
especially when she's wearing her black tutu,
and she can't wait to see a real show at the
theatre with the rest of her class.

But when the curtain rises,
where is Pink Rabbit?

Love Isadora Moon?
Why not try these too . . .

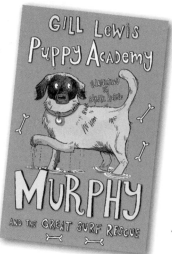